The Fun House

Jill McDougall
Photographs by Lindsay Edwards

Contents

A Place to Play 2
Slides and Tunnels 4
Jump, Jump, Jump! 8
Fun for Little Children 10
The Climbing Wall 12
The Party Room 14
Glossary 16

A Place to Play

The fun house is a place in the city
where children can go to play.

Inside the fun house, girls and boys
can slide, jump and climb.

Some families like to go to the fun house
on rainy days.
Children can play and have fun
without getting wet in the rain.

Slides and Tunnels

There are some slides in the fun house.

The long slides are for children who like to go down them very fast.

The little slides are for small children.
They can go down slowly
so they don't feel scared.

All children must sit down to ride
on the slides.

There are lots of tunnels
in the fun house.

Some tunnels are for children
to slide down.
These tunnels have twists and turns
to make the ride more fun.

One tunnel is on the ground.
Small children can crawl along this tunnel and come out at the end.

Jump, Jump, Jump!

At the back of the fun house, there are places just for jumping.

The trampolines are for bigger children. Sometimes, the big children do tricks on these trampolines.

There are nets around the outside so that no one gets hurt.

Near the trampolines,
there is a big **jumping castle**.

Smaller children have fun jumping here.

Fun for Little Children

There is a place beside the tunnels for very small children to play.

They can ride on tiny trucks that have funny faces on them.

Some little girls and boys
play in the **ball pit**.

They like to roll around on the little balls
inside the pit.

The Climbing Wall

There is a big **climbing wall**
in the fun house.

Children can climb all the way
to the top of the wall.

Little rocks are stuck to the climbing wall.
Children put their hands and feet
on the rocks to help them climb up.

The Party Room

Children can have a birthday party
at the fun house.

There is a room behind the trampolines
called the party room.

In this room, there is a long table
for party food.

Big children and small children
can all have a good time
at the fun house.

HAPPY BIRTHDAY HAPPY BIRTHDAY HAPPY BIRTHD

Glossary

ball pit a big hole with little balls in it

climbing wall
a wall with little rocks for climbing up

jumping castle
a blow-up house for children to jump on